Note to parents, carers and teachers

Read it yourself is a series of modern stories, favourite characters and traditional tales written in a simple way for children who are learning to read. The books can be read independently or as part of a guided reading session.

Each book is carefully structured to include many high-frequency words vital for first reading. The sentences on each page are supported closely by pictures to help with understanding, and to offer lively details to talk about.

The books are graded into four levels that progressively introduce wider vocabulary and longer stories as a reader's ability and confidence grows.

Ideas for use

- Begin by looking through the book and talking about the pictures. Has your child heard this story before?

- Help your child with any words he does not know, either by helping him to sound them out or supplying them yourself.

- Developing readers can be concentrating so hard on the words that they sometimes don't fully grasp the meaning of what they're reading. Answering the puzzle questions on pages 30 and 31 will help with understanding.

For more information and advice on Read it yourself and book banding, visit www.ladybird.com/readityourself

Book
Band
6

Level 2 is ideal for children who have received some reading instruction and can read short, simple sentences with help.

Special features:

Frequent repetition of main story words and phrases

Short, simple sentences

There was a man who had three daughters.

Beauty was the youngest daughter and she was good and kind.

Large, clear type

One day, the man had to go away.

"Would you like me to bring you back a present?" he said to his three daughters.

Careful match between story and pictures

Educational Consultant: Geraldine Taylor
Book Banding Consultant: Kate Ruttle

A catalogue record for this book is available from the British Library

Published by Ladybird Books Ltd
80 Strand, London, WC2R 0RL
A Penguin Company

001

ISBN: 978-0-72327-508-4

Printed in China

Beauty and the Beast

Illustrated by
Marsela Hajdinjak-Krec

There was a man
who had three daughters.

Beauty was the youngest
daughter and she was
good and kind.

One day, the man had to go away.

"Would you like me to bring you back a present?" he said to his three daughters.

"Please bring me back a necklace," said the first daughter.

"Please bring me back a ring," said the second daughter.

"Please bring me back a rose," said Beauty, the youngest daughter.

One day, when the man was away, he saw a castle. The castle had roses in the garden.

"I have a necklace and ring, so I will now take a rose as a present for Beauty," said the man.

"Do not take the roses!" said a beast.

"Do not hurt me!"
said the man.

"No," said the beast, "I will
not hurt you. But you must
now bring me back the
first thing you see when
you get home."

When the man got home, the first thing he saw was Beauty.

As she was good and kind, Beauty said, "Father, I will go to stay with the beast."

The beast was kind to
Beauty and Beauty liked
the beast.

One day, the beast asked
Beauty to marry him.

"No," said Beauty.
"I like you, but I will not
marry you."

One day, Beauty went to stay with her father.

When Beauty got back to the castle, the first thing she saw was the beast. He was ill.

"Please do not be ill,"
Beauty said to the beast,
"I do love you."

The beast became a prince.

"You have broken the spell," he said.

The prince asked Beauty to marry him.

"Yes," said Beauty. "I do love you and I will marry you!"

How much do you remember about the story of Beauty and the Beast? Answer these questions and find out!

- How many daughters does the man have?

- What does Beauty ask the man to bring back?

- What is the first thing the man sees when he gets home?

- What happens when Beauty says she loves the beast?

Look at the pictures and match them to the story words.

Beauty

beast

rose

man

castle

prince

Read it yourself with Ladybird

Tick the books you've read!

For beginner readers who can read short, simple sentences with help.

Level 2

- Beauty and the Beast ☐
- Chicken Licken ☐
- Little Red Riding Hood ☐
- Nature Trail ☐
- Sports Day ☐
- Pirate School ☐
- Rumpelstiltskin ☐
- Sleeping Beauty ☐
- The Gingerbread Man ☐
- Sly Fox and Red Hen ☐
- The Tale of Jemima Puddle-Duck ☐
- The Three Little Pigs ☐
- Why Lion Roarrrs! ☐
- Topsy and Tim: The Big Race ☐
- Town Mouse and Country Mouse ☐
- Dom's Dragon ☐

For more confident readers who can read simple stories with help.

Level 3

- YOU won't like this present as much as I DO! ☐
- The Elves and the Shoemaker ☐
- Hansel and Gretel ☐
- Harry and the Bucketful of Dinosaurs ☐
- Jack and the Beanstalk ☐
- Furi on Music Island ☐
- Poppet Stows Away ☐
- Rapunzel ☐
- The Red Knight ☐